Colors of Creation

Thomas Paul Thigpen
Illustrated by Jane Conteh-Morgan

Chariot Books™
David C. Cook Publishing Co.

S0-AAK-114

BLACK is where the world began:
a silent space,
an empty place,
till light appeared at God's command
to form the night and day.

WHITE God scattered out like pearls
across the sky,
where comets fly.
God spoke and made a million worlds:
the stars, the Milky Way.

BLUE spread out a covering
with foamy lace
on earth's new face.
God's Spirit there was hovering
above the ocean waves.

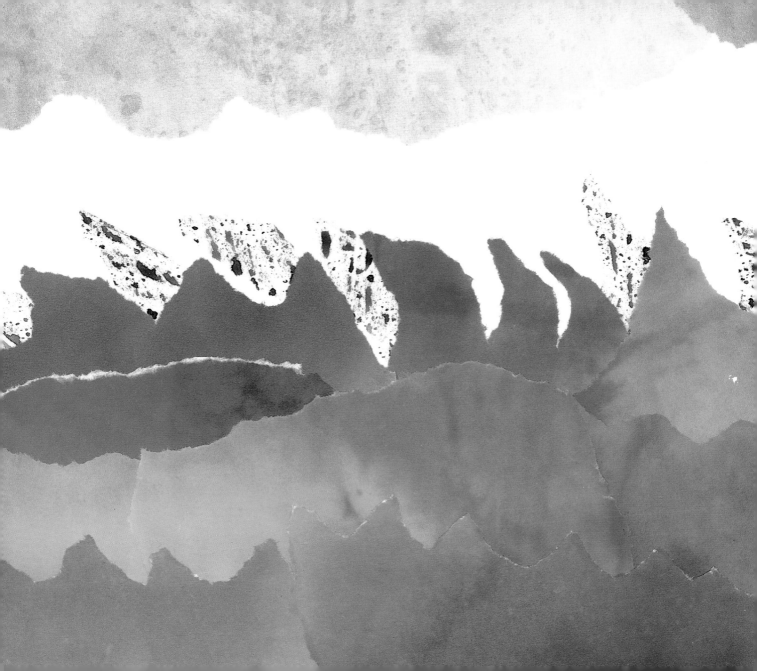

BROWN rose up to form the land.
Out of the tides
climbed mountainsides.
God shaped with stone and clay and sand
the valleys, hills, and caves.

GREEN soon sprouted everywhere:
the mighty pine,
the twisting vine,
the willow tree with wispy hair,
the grasses of the plain.

YELLOW brightly, boldly grew:
across the hills
laughed daffodils,
daisies, dandelions, too,
and bursting yellow grain.

PURPLE painted fruits grew sweet:
the plum's dark shape,
the clustered grape.
The eggplant and the humble beet
swelled full and ripe and round.

ORANGE sun now ruled the day
while full-moon light
ruled over night.
Orange fish in stream and bay,
deep sea and shallow sound.

RED came winging through the air
on robin's breast,
on cardinal's crest.
While red fur warmed the fox's lair
and gleamed on setter's coat.

GRAY appeared on elephant's tail,
on hippo's hide
and rhino's side,
on playful porpoise, gentle whale
and possums' furry throats.

Then when the earth at last was full
of creatures small
and broad and tall,
with fin and feather, skin and wool,
God said, "I have work still."

Who will fill the world with song
and crown the days
with prayer and praise?
Who will know the right from wrong,
and seek to do my will?

So God formed people from the dust
to work and play
to love and pray
and all the creatures gave to us
to be our friends and food.

God liked each color, fresh and new
the pale, the bright,
the dark, the light
so people came in every hue,
and God said: This is good!